A Note to Parents and Caregivers:

Read-it! Readers are for children who are just starting on the amazing road to reading. These beautiful books support both the acquisition of reading skills and the love of books.

The PURPLE LEVEL presents basic topics and objects using high frequency words and simple language patterns.

The RED LEVEL presents familiar topics using common words and repeating sentence patterns.

The BLUE LEVEL presents new ideas using a larger vocabulary and varied sentence structure.

The YELLOW LEVEL presents more challenging ideas, a broad vocabulary, and wide variety in sentence structure.

The GREEN LEVEL presents more complex ideas, an extended vocabulary range, and expanded language structures.

The ORANGE LEVEL presents a wide range of ideas and concepts using challenging vocabulary and complex language structures.

When sharing a book with your child, read in short stretches, pausing often to talk about the pictures. Have your child turn the pages and point to the pictures and familiar words. And be sure to reread favorite stories or parts of stories.

There is no right or wrong way to share books with children. Find time to read with your child, and pass on the legacy of literacy.

Adria F. Klein, Ph.D.
Professor Emeritus
California State University
San Bernardino, California

Editor: Christianne Jones
Designer: Joe Anderson
Page Production: Tracy Kaehler
Creative Director: Keith Griffin
Editorial Director: Carol Jones
The illustrations in this book were created digitally.

Picture Window Books
5115 Excelsior Boulevard
Suite 232
Minneapolis, MN 55416
877-845-8392
www.picturewindowbooks.com

Printed in the United States of America.

Library of Congress Cataloging-in-Publication Data
Blackaby, Susan.
The missing tooth / by Susan Blackaby ; illustrated by Ryan Haugen.
p. cm. — (Read-it! readers)
Summary: Kim has a bad morning when she wakes up late and loses a tooth, but the
next morning she feels much better.
ISBN 1-4048-1592-9 (hardcover)
[1. Teeth—Fiction. 2. Mood (Psychology)—Fiction.] I. Haugen, Ryan, 1972-, ill.
II. Title. III. Series.

PZ7.B5318Mis 2005
[E]—dc22

2005021449

The Missing Tooth

by Susan Blackaby
illustrated by Ryan Haugen

Special thanks to our advisers for their expertise:

Adria F. Klein, Ph.D.
Professor Emeritus, California State University
San Bernardino, California

Susan Kesselring, M.A.
Literacy Educator
Rosemount–Apple Valley–Eagan (Minnesota) School District

PiCTURE WiNDOW BOOKS
Minneapolis, Minnesota

Kim woke up late.
"Oh, no," said Kim.

She poked a hole in her sock.
"Oh, no," mumbled Kim.

Kim tripped over her cat.

"Oh, no!" cried Kim.

9

Kim bit into her apple. "OH, NO!
I lost a tooth!" yelled Kim.

11

Kim felt sad. She thought she looked like a jack-o'-lantern.

13

Kim met Jan on the bus.

Jan grinned.

Kim felt glad. Jan had a missing tooth, too.

That night, Kim got ready for bed.

She brushed carefully around her missing tooth.

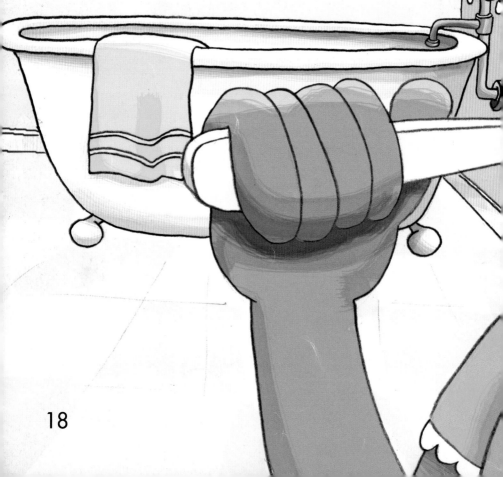

Then, Kim put her tooth under
her pillow.

Dear
Tooth
Fairy

Kim

21

The next day, Kim woke up right on time. She found a surprise under her pillow. Kim felt happy.

More *Read-it!* Readers

Bright pictures and fun stories help you practice your reading skills. Look for more books at your level.

Ann Plants a Garden 1-4048-1010-2
The Babysitter 1-4048-1187-7
Bess and Tess 1-4048-1013-7
The Best Soccer Player 1-4048-1055-2
Dan Gets Set 1-4048-1011-0
Fishing Trip 1-4048-1004-8
Jen Plays 1-4048-1008-0
Joey's First Day 1-4048-1174-5
Just Try It 1-4048-1175-3
Mary's Art 1-4048-1056-0
Moving Day 1-4048-1006-4
Pat Picks Up 1-4048-1059-5
A Place for Mike 1-4048-1012-9
Room to Share 1-4048-1185-0
Shopping for Lunch 1-4048-1589-9
Syd's Room 1-4048-1585-6
Wes Gets a Pet 1-4048-1060-9
Winter Fun for Kat 1-4048-1007-2
A Year of Fun 1-4048-1009-9

Looking for a specific title or level? A complete list of *Read-it!* Readers is available on our Web site:
www.picturewindowbooks.com